OLAF'S INCREDIBLE
MACHINE

by Nicholas Brennan

Windmill Books and E. P. Dutton

To Patrick Hardy and Lance Salway
who helped so much with this book.

First published in the U.S.A. 1975 by
Windmill Books and E. P. Dutton

Copyright © 1973 by Nicholas Brennan

LIBRARY OF CONGRESS CATALOGING IN PUBLICATION DATA

Brennan, Nicholas   Olaf's incredible machine

SUMMARY: When the machine he invents grows so
large that it threatens to take over the world,
Olaf decides to get away from it all in his balloon.

[1. Pollution—Fiction]   I. Title.
PZ7.B75164Ol4   [E]   74-16386   ISBN 0-525-61008-1

Printed in Belgium by Offset-Printing Van den Bossche ⓜ

Professor Olaf was an inventor. He invented machines, some of which were useful and some of which were not. One day, he invented an <u>incredible</u> machine.

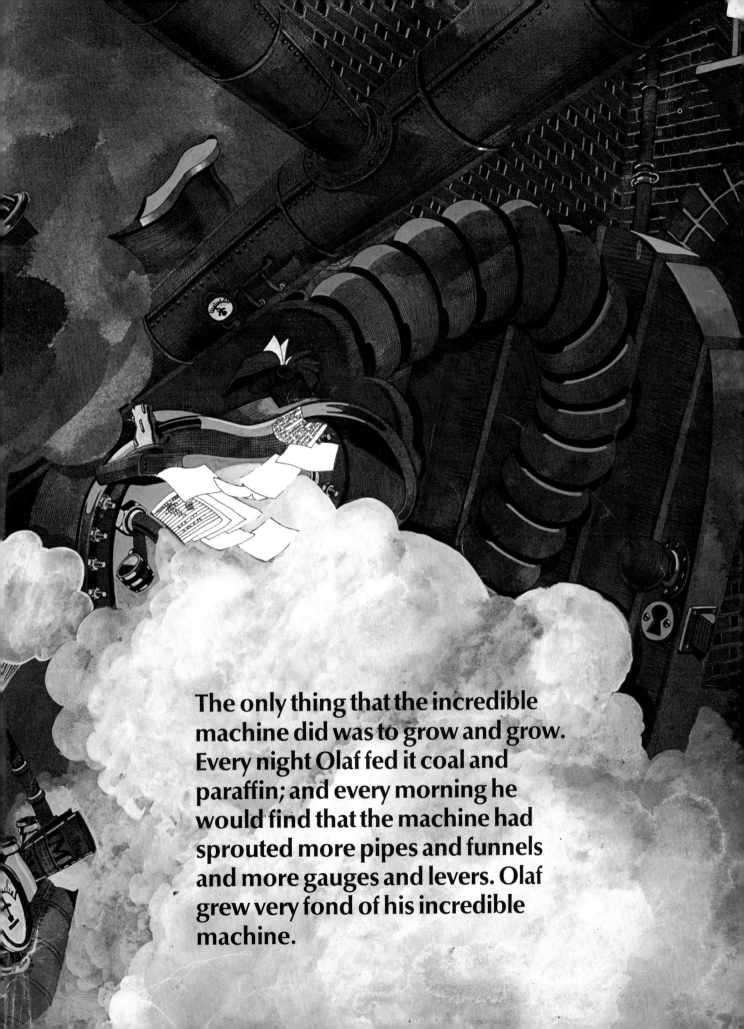

The only thing that the incredible machine did was to grow and grow. Every night Olaf fed it coal and paraffin; and every morning he would find that the machine had sprouted more pipes and funnels and more gauges and levers. Olaf grew very fond of his incredible machine.

The machine grew and grew and became so big that Olaf couldn't manage it by himself. So he hired men to help him and he built long rows of houses for them all to live in. And still the machine grew across the countryside and the smoke and the fumes became thicker and stronger.

Before long, Olaf and the workmen and their houses were covered in thick smoke, and still the machine grew and grew. Olaf became very worried. He knew that the machine had grown much too big. But he had forgotten to invent a way of stopping it from growing, and the workmen were all too busy to pay any attention to him.

So Olaf decided to leave them with his machine and all the smoke. He made an enormous balloon with a platform, and he loaded plants and animals on to it.

And then he sailed up into the fresh, clean air and left it all behind.

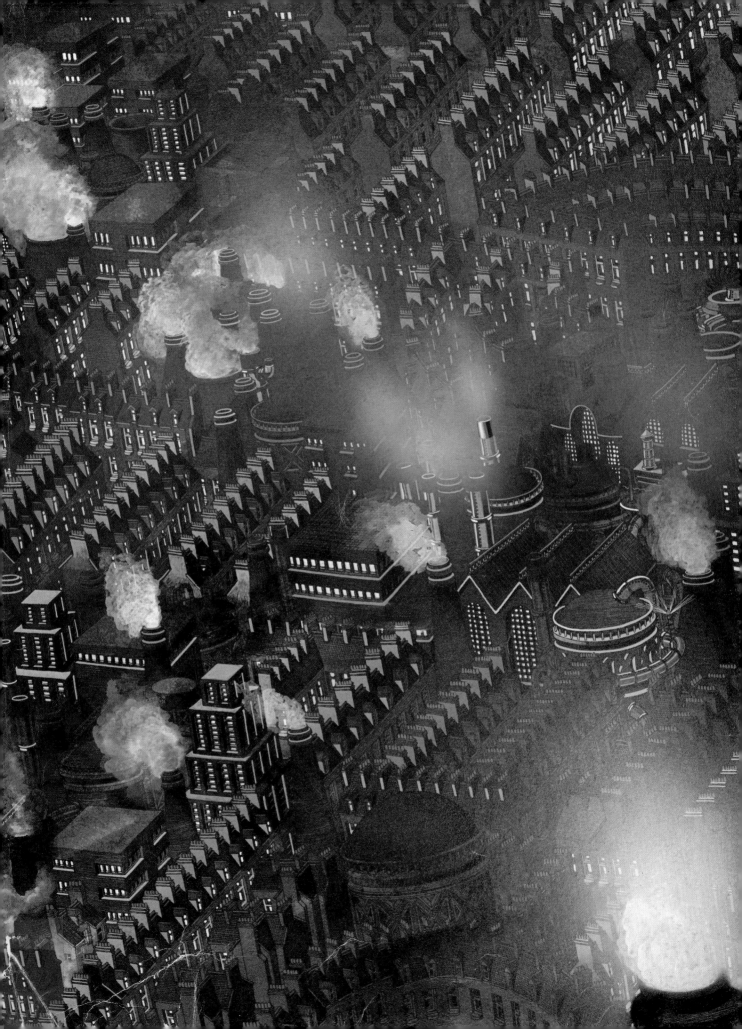

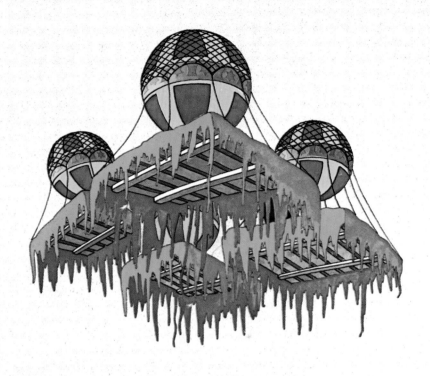

The plants began to grow in the fresh air and the animals thrived. Olaf built more balloons and more platforms and his balloon-land grew larger and larger. He looked down on the smoke below and was glad to be away from it all.

As time went by, the roots and tendrils of the plants grew longer and longer until they reached down to the smoke-filled town below. One day, a boy saw one of the tendrils and climbed up into Olaf's beautiful balloon-land. Other people followed him and Olaf was happy to let them stay in his country. As more and more people arrived, Olaf had to build more and more platforms and balloons.

Before long there was nobody left below in the town. And the incredible machine at last came to a stop because there was no one to look after it and no one to feed it with coal and paraffin.

But the weight of all the people and the plants and the animals became too great for the beautiful balloons that Olaf had built. The platforms creaked and groaned and then Olaf's world fell to the ground with an enormous crash.

It fell right on top of the town and covered it completely. The houses and the smoke and the incredible machine all disappeared and the earth was fresh and green again.

And Olaf started to think about his next invention . . .